The Three Blind Mice Mystery

CASE:
MISSING
MOUSE

The Three Blind Mice Mystery

by STEPHEN KRENSKY

illustrated by **Lynn Munsinger**

A Yearling First Choice Chapter Book

For David

— S.K.

Published by Bantam Doubleday Dell Publishing Group, Inc.
1540 Broadway
New York, New York 10036
Text copyright © 1995 by Stephen Krensky
Illustrations copyright © 1995 by Lynn Munsinger
All rights reserved.

Library of Congress Cataloging-in-Publication Data
Krensky, Stephen.
 The three blind mice mystery / by Stephen Krensky ; illustrated by
Lynn Munsinger.
  p. cm.
 Summary: Simple Simon plays detective as he becomes involved with
a variety of nursery rhyme characters in his attempt to locate two
missing blind mice.
 Hardcover ISBN 0-385-32131-7 — Paperback ISBN 0-440-41082-7
 [1. Mystery and detective stories. 2. Mice—Fiction.]
I. Munsinger, Lynn, ill. II. Title.
PZ7.K883Th 1995
[E]—dc20   94-32511 CIP AC

Hardcover: The trademark Delacorte Press® is registered in the
U.S. Patent and Trademark Office and in other countries.

Paperback: The trademarks Yearling® and Dell® are registered in the
U.S. Patent and Trademark Office and in other countries.

The text of this book is set in 17-point Baskerville.

Manufactured in the United States of America

October 1995   10 9 8 7 6 5 4 3 2

CONTENTS

1. A Missing Mouse

I was sitting at home one afternoon
thinking about pies.
Blueberry and apple
and cherry and chocolate cream.
I love pies.

There was a knock at my door.

Albert burst in.

He was one of the three blind mice.

They lived across the meadow.

"Hello, Albert," I said.

"Simple Simon!" he cried.

"Thank goodness I found you."

Actually, my name is just plain Simon.

The pieman called me

Simple Simon first.

He said I would do *simply* anything

to get a pie.

After that, the name stuck.

"What happened?" I asked.

I already knew something was wrong.

Detectives like myself can always tell.

"It's Charlie," said Albert.

"He is missing!"

Charlie was Albert's younger brother.

Benjamin was the one in the middle.

"Come home with me," said Albert.

"There is no time to waste."

I followed Albert back
across the meadow.
We almost bumped into a wolf
on the way.

The wolf was in a big hurry.

He paid no attention to us.

"I will show them," he muttered,

brushing some straw from his shoulders.

When we arrived at the mouse house,

Benjamin was pacing in the living room.

"Oh, dear!" he squeaked.

"First that farmer's wife cut off our tails

with a carving knife.

And now this!"

"How long has Charlie been gone?"

I asked. "A day? A week?"

"An hour," said Albert.

He sank into a chair.

"Oh," I said.

"An hour is not very long.
Maybe he just wandered off."
Benjamin shook his head.
"Charlie would never leave
without telling us," he said.
"Besides, it all happened so fast.
One minute Charlie was sitting
on the porch.
The next minute he was gone."

I took out my casebook to make notes.

Detectives need to look professional.

"Did you notice anything unusual?"

I asked.

Albert shook his head.

"I only heard the wind," said Benjamin.

"Oh, dear! Oh, dear!

Do you think he was mousenapped?"

I did not know what to think yet.

That's why it was a mystery.

2. The Hungry Wolf

I told Albert and Benjamin not to worry.

Detectives always say that.

It makes everyone feel better.

Then I went outside to look for clues.

The porch was bare

except for some straw.

The yard was muddy
because it had rained
during the night.
If there had been
mousenappers,
they would have
made footprints.
I saw none.

There was more straw, though.
I drew some of it in my casebook.
At that moment,
a ball landed at my feet.
Two children came up to get it.
I recognized them at once.
Detectives need to have good memories.

The children were part of a big family.

They lived in a shoe nearby.

"Hello, Jack and Jill," I said.

I asked them about Charlie.

"We have not seen him," said Jill.

"But Mother might have," said Jack.

"She does not miss much."

I found their mother
putting clothes out to dry.
"Laundry and more laundry,"
she sighed.
"I have so many children.
Sometimes I don't know what to do."
I helped her unload her basket.
"Have you seen anything funny lately?"
I asked.

"Just that wolf," she said.

"He has been around for a few days.

Stays in the woods at night."

She put the last shirt in the basket.

"Will you stay for supper, Simon?

We are having pie for dessert."

"Yes, Ma'am," I said.

Detectives always think better

on a full stomach.

After supper,

I made my way to the woods.

Maybe this wolf knew something.

I found him doing sit-ups

against a fallen log.

"Ninety-eight, ninety-nine . . . ,"

huffed the wolf.

"Excuse me," I said.

"One hundred," the wolf finished.

He jumped up

and began running in place.

"I am looking for a missing mouse,"
I said.

"Mouse?" The wolf made a face.

"I do not bother with mice. Too small."
He licked his lips.

"I like pigs better."

"Maybe you saw—" I began.

"I am busy!" the wolf snapped.

"Can't you see that?"

I could see he had an awful lot of teeth.

All that exercise was making him hungry.

Detectives learn to pay attention.

Clearly, it was time to leave.

I went home to bed,
but I did not sleep well.
I kept dreaming of a wolf
cooking mice in a big pot.

3. A Noisy Wind

The next morning, I went back
to check on Albert and Benjamin.
I found Albert sitting alone on the stairs.
"Good morning," I said.
"It is not good at all," Albert replied.
"It is terrible.
Now Benjamin is gone too."

Detectives should be prepared

for anything.

Still, I was surprised.

"Tell me what happened," I said.

"I was making breakfast," said Albert.

"Benjamin was sitting on the porch.

I heard a clattering noise.

I asked Benjamin if he heard it too."

Albert took a deep breath.

"He never answered.

When I came out he was gone."

"Did you notice anything this time?"

I asked.

"Just the clattering," said Albert,

"and a really strong gust of wind."

I looked around.

The front yard was covered with sticks.

That explained the
clattering,

but where had the

sticks come from?

I drew one of them

in my casebook.

CASE: MISSING
~~MOUSE~~
MICE

stick

Just then, I heard

loud voices arguing in the road.

I went out to investigate.

"You have no proof,"

the wolf was saying.

"Oh, yes, I do," said Mother Goose.

"The pigs told me themselves."

The wolf snorted.

"Pigs will say anything!" he said.

28

"Now, if you'll excuse me,
I have to save my breath."
Mother Goose watched
the wolf slink away.
"I am sure he did it," she said.
"Yesterday, he blew down
the first pig's house of straw.

And this morning, he blew down
the second pig's house of sticks.
Luckily, both pigs escaped.
They are in their brother's brick house."
She pointed. "It's the one over there."
I asked her about Charlie and Benjamin,
but she just shook her head.

On a hunch,

I decided to visit the pigs.

Detectives like to get hunches.

I knocked at the door of the brick house.

All three pigs looked out the window.

Then they opened up.

"I am looking for two missing mice,"

I explained.

"We haven't seen anything,"

said the third little pig.

"We have been too busy with the wolf."

I could understand that.

"By the way," I added,

"when the wolf blew down your houses,

was there a lot of wind?"

"Like a hurricane,"

said the first little pig.

"That wolf can really huff and puff,"

said the second little pig.

"But we'll be safe here,"

said the third little pig.

"Good luck," I said.

"And be careful."

I went back to where
the two pig houses had stood.
Some straw and sticks were still
on the ground.
I checked them against the drawings
in my casebook.
They both matched perfectly.

34

Then I drew a map in my casebook.

It showed where both houses had been.

"Very interesting," I thought.

Now I knew how the mice had vanished.

I just did not know where they had gone.

4. Lost and Found

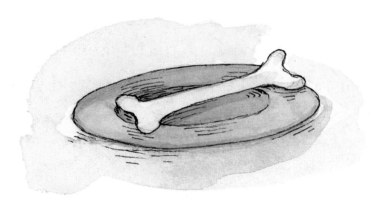

I was on my way to tell Albert
what I had learned.
Suddenly, I saw Old Mother Hubbard
running toward me.
"Robbed!" she shouted.
"I have been robbed!"
"Give me the facts," I said.
Detectives love facts.

She took a deep breath.

"Yesterday, I went to my cupboard.

I was getting my poor dog a bone.

The cupboard was bare, though.

So I went shopping.

When I got back

there was straw all over the place.

I put the groceries away and cleaned up."

"Did you close the cupboard doors?"
I asked.

"Of course," she said. "Good and tight.
Then, this morning,
I opened the cupboard again.
A lot of the food was gone!
And then, the next thing I knew,
the wind picked up.
Guess what happened next?"

Detectives do not get to smile often.

"Sticks came flying
through your window," I said.

"Why, yes," she said.

"It made quite a mess."

"Have you looked in the cupboard
again?" I asked.

"Well, no," she said.

"The second wind blew
the doors shut again, while
I was busy cleaning up the kitchen."

"We should look in the cupboard now,"
I said.

"What about the food thief?" she asked.

"Do not worry," I said.

"We will get to the bottom of this."

When we arrived at her house,
we heard noises inside the cupboard.

"What could that be?"
asked Old Mother Hubbard.

"I think I know," I said.

I opened the cupboard.

Charlie and Benjamin looked out.

"About time you showed up,"
said Charlie.
"There is nothing left to eat here,
and this door was stuck."
Benjamin just burped.

5. Pie at Last

A short while later,
the mice were all back home.
We were having tea
with Old Mother Hubbard.
"So you were the food thief, Charlie,"
she said.

"It was not my fault," he said.
Charlie explained that the sudden wind
had caught him by surprise.
"Of course," I said.
"You did not know the wolf
was blowing down the first pig's house."
Charlie nodded.
"The wind picked me up
and turned me around and around.

44

I landed in the cupboard,
and I hit my head.
I didn't know where I was.
My head ached terribly.
So I crawled into a corner
and fell asleep."

He looked at Old Mother Hubbard.

"I guess you missed me
when you filled the cupboard.
When I woke up, it was dark.
I was hungry.
There were plenty of things to eat.
After dinner, I went back to the corner
and slept some more.
The next think I knew,
I heard a loud thump."

"The thump was me," said Benjamin,
rubbing his shoulder.

"Because of the wolf again," I said.

"At that moment,
he was blowing down the house of sticks."

Albert poured more tea.

"Well, all's well that ends well," he said.

His brothers nodded.

I never charge for my services,
but the mice baked me
three very nice pies.
And Old Mother Hubbard
had me over for supper twice.
You may be wondering
what finally happened
to the three little pigs.
Well, that's another story.